MOONWALK

Sean Callery and Emil Dacanay

Evans

Contents

Man on the Moon 6

We have lift-off! 8

Worried dad 10

The race to the Moon 12

Fuel low 14

The Eagle has landed 16

One small step 18

Kangaroo hops! 20

Scary moment 22

Front page news 24

Splashdown 26

More Moon visits 28

Glossary 31

Webography 31

Index 31

Man on the Moon

Hi, I'm Jay. My dad is helping men get to the Moon for the first time.

In 1969 the first men went to the Moon, a ball of rock that goes round the Earth. They were Neil Armstrong and Buzz Aldrin. A third man, Michael Collins, stayed in the spacecraft so that they could get back.

We have lift-off!

We could not hear our own voices as the Saturn 5 rocket took off.

The sound of the rocket is the loudest noise man has ever made! Saturn 5 is blasting 68km (42 miles) up against the Earth's gravity into space at a speed of more than 9,600 km/h (6,000 mph)!

Worried dad

Thursday July 17

Dad said, "The plan is working so far. I hope nothing goes wrong."

Apollo 11 plan

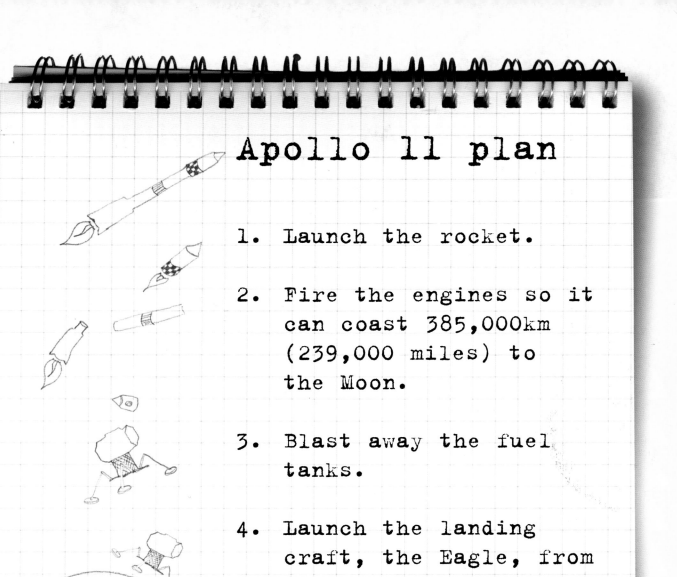

1. Launch the rocket.

2. Fire the engines so it can coast 385,000km (239,000 miles) to the Moon.

3. Blast away the fuel tanks.

4. Launch the landing craft, the Eagle, from the command module, Columbia.

5. Land on the Moon.

6. Fly back up to the command module.

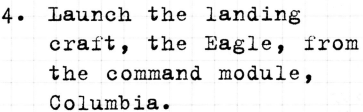

7. Return to Earth.

The race to the Moon

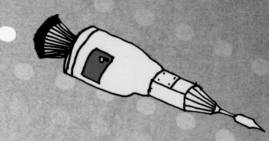

Saturday July 19

Dad told me these were not the
first men in space.

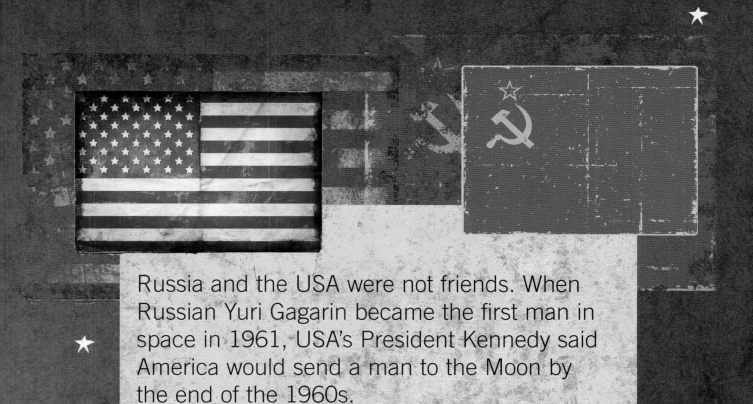

Russia and the USA were not friends. When Russian Yuri Gagarin became the first man in space in 1961, USA's President Kennedy said America would send a man to the Moon by the end of the 1960s.

Fuel low

Sunday July 20

Dad took me to work with him.
"You can be my lucky mascot,"
he said.
Then his face went pale.
"They're low on fuel."

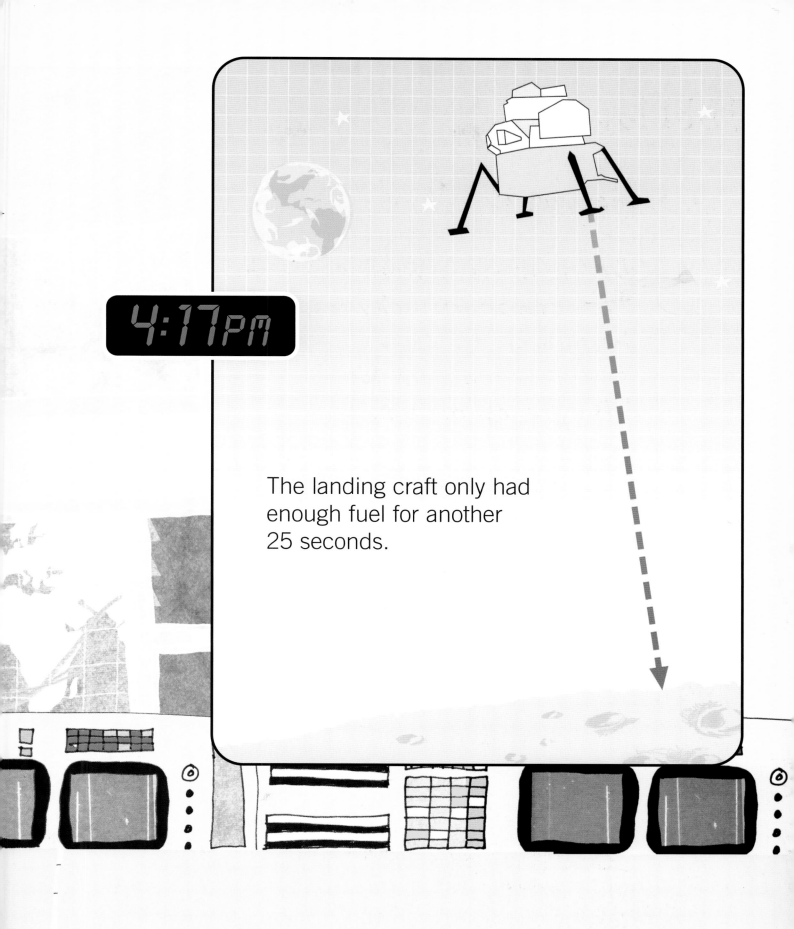

4:17pm

The landing craft only had enough fuel for another 25 seconds.

The Eagle has landed

Dad wiped his forehead.
"That was close. You
brought us luck, Jay!"

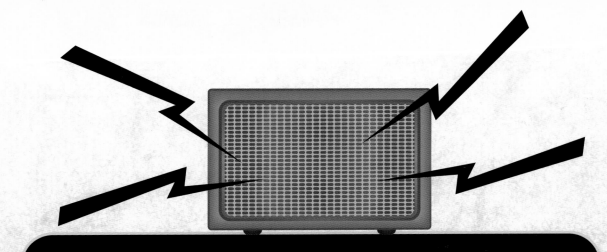

"OK, engine stop,"

said Buzz Aldrin.

Neil Armstrong said,

"The Eagle has landed."

Dad's boss said:

"We're breathing again!"

One small step

Monday July 21

We watched a fuzzy
TV picture as Armstrong
climbed down
the ladder.

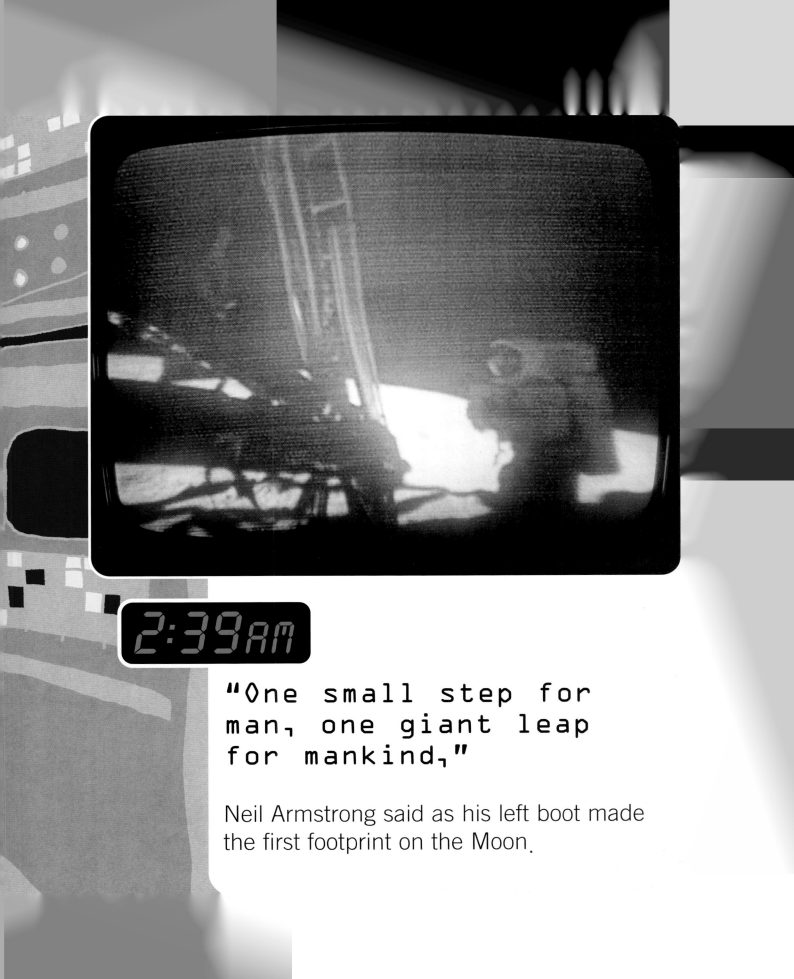

2:39AM

"One small step for man, one giant leap for mankind,"

Neil Armstrong said as his left boot made the first footprint on the Moon.

Kangaroo hops!

The Moon's gravity is so weak that the astronauts hop up and float down to move about. It looks fun!

9:00AM

Armstrong and Aldrin collected rocks and dust and planted an American flag.

Scary moment

Monday July 21

Dad went pale again.
"The switch broke.
The engines won't fire," he said.
Were they stuck on the Moon?

5:54pm

Buzz Aldrin pushed a felt tip pen
in to work the switch. The engines fired.

Front page news

Dad fell asleep over the newspaper!

Boy helper

Wednesday July 23

Dad said, "A ten-year-old boy helped us to keep in contact with Columbia!" I felt a bit jealous.

MAN WALKS ON THE MOON

TUESDAY JULY 22

Historic milestone in space

Astronaut Neil Armstrong stepped from the lunar module at 2.39am yesterday morning.

Captain M

Gl

10:30pm

At the tracking station in Guam a part got stuck. Head man Charles Force got his son Greg to fix it because his small hands fitted in the gap.

Splashdown

When we saw Columbia floating in the sea,
Dad shook hands with everyone, even me!

USSR

CANADA

USA

CHINA

JAPAN

PHILIPPINES

✕ HAWAII

PAPUA NEW GUINEA

AUSTRALIA

NEW ZEALAND

The spacecraft splashed into the Pacific Ocean and soon the astronauts were safe.

More Moon visits

Friday July 25

I stared at the Moon.
I want to be an astronaut.

There were five more
successful trips to the Moon.

One day we could go
on holiday there!

Mission	Launch date	Notes
Apollo 12	November 14 1969	Rocket was hit by a bolt of lightning
Apollo 13	April 11 1970	Did not land as the spacecraft was damaged
Apollo 14	January 31 1971	Used a cart to collect rocks
Apollo 15	July 26 1971	Stayed for three days
Apollo 16	April 16 1972	Used the lunar rover vehicle
Apollo 17	December 7 1972	The last trip to the Moon

Glossary

Astronaut: person who travels in a spacecraft
Command Module: the spacecraft (called Columbia) that orbited round the Moon
Gravity: the force that pulls us down onto Earth
Landing Craft: the spacecraft that landed on the Moon
Orbit: the path an object takes when it goes round a star, planet or moon

Webography

http://history.nasa.gov/ap11ann/kippsphotos/apollo.html
You can view a collection of photos relating to the Apollo 11
mission to the Moon at this website.

http://news.nationalgeographic.com/news/2009/07/090715-moon-landing-apollo-facts.html
The National Geographic's web pages are full of facts about the
Apollo 11 Moon landing.

http://idahoptv.org/dialogue4kids/season6/moon/facts.cfm
This website is packed with information about Earth's Moon.

Index

Aldrin, Buzz 7, 17, 21, 23
America 13, 21
Apollo 11 11
Armstrong, Neil 7, 17, 18, 19, 21, 25
astronaut 25, 27, 28
Collins, Michael 7
Columbia 11, 24, 26
command module 11
Eagle, The 11, 16, 17

footprint 19
Gagarin, Yuri 13
gravity 9, 20
landing craft 11, 15
Pacific Ocean 27
Russia 13
Saturn 5 8, 9
USA 13

If you enjoyed this book, look out for another Take 2 title:

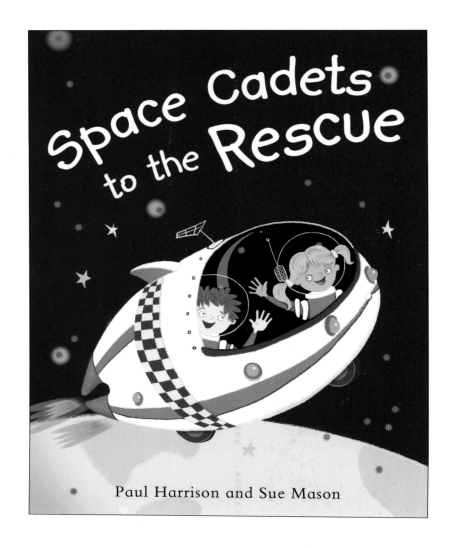

Space Cadets to the Rescue

Paul Harrison and Sue Mason

a fun story about two brave young space rangers who have to fight off an alien attack.